THE STRANGE CASE OF
DR. JEKYLL
AND MR. HYDE

The Young Collector's Illustrated Classics

THE STRANGE CASE OF DR. JEKYLL AND MR. HYDE

By
Robert Louis Stevenson

Adapted by
Stacy Savran

Illustrated by
Eva Clift

Cover Art by
Richard Martin

Contents

Chapter 1

BLACKMAIL HOUSE

*M*r. Gabriel John Utterson was a man of few words and rare smiles. One would surely think such an unfriendly character would be lacking in companionship. Oddly enough, however, Mr. Utterson kept a close-knit circle of friends who were quite at ease in his presence. They found him to be accepting of others' misdeeds and, in most cases, willing to help the wrongdoer. He was never one to criticize.

Like many lawyers, Mr. Utterson counted as friends his relatives and others he had known for a long time. And so it was that Mr. Richard Enfield, a well-known man about town, was both Mr. Utterson's cousin and friend.

Each Sunday, the two friends took a leisurely walk around the city of London. Townspeople who encountered them reported that not a word would pass between the two—and one would look as bored as the other! Yet, the lawyer and his young cousin continued to take these excursions. They even avoided business calls so they would not be interrupted. It remained a mystery to all.

It was on one of these silent Sunday strolls that the lawyer and his cousin chanced upon a quiet side street in a busy quarter of London. The street was unlike the others in its dingy neighborhood. With freshly painted shutters and general cleanliness, it was a welcome sight to passersby.

Upon nearing the corner, the amblers came across an old, two-story building with no windows. Its filthy walls and cracked moldings revealed

obvious neglect. And it looked remarkably sinister in its spotless surroundings. The pair stopped and stared, neither man able take his eyes off it.

Mr. Enfield lifted up his walking cane and pointed it towards the building's battered, weatherbeaten door. "Have you ever seen that door?" he asked Mr. Utterson, a sudden look of horror flashing across his face.

"Indeed I have," replied Mr. Utterson. "But to me it is just a door. I can see by the look on your face that it means a great deal more than that to you."

"Oh yes...one frightful night I encountered that door, my good man," Mr. Enfield said in a husky voice.

Mr. Utterson's usually indifferent tone took on a note of nervous curiosity. "Please, go on," he urged. He knew something dreadful must have happened to have shaken his young cousin so.

Glancing over his shoulder to

make sure they were alone, Mr. Enfield began his chilling tale. "Well, it goes like this," he whispered. "I was walking home from a party very late one evening. The streets were empty of people but full of lamps flooding with light. Everyone, or almost everyone, was asleep in their beds.

"As I neared an intersection not far from here," Mr. Enfield continued, "I saw a little man stomping towards me on the sidewalk across the street. At the same moment, I witnessed a young girl of eight or ten running as hard as she could down the cross street. Where either of them were racing at that hour I cannot imagine. But fate stepped in their tracks when the two ran right into each other at the corner. The child was knocked to the ground."

The lawyer shook his head in disbelief and muttered, "Dear oh dear. But how is this tragic thing connected to that door?"

"You'll understand in a moment—I am just getting to the real tragedy," said Mr. Enfield. "The man, who'd had the wind knocked out of him but was still left standing, trampled over the fallen girl's body and began to run away as she screamed!"

Completely shocked and at a loss for words, Mr. Utterson turned quite pale. His usually solid core felt like it had just taken a few strong blows, as if he had been knocked off his own feet.

Mr. Enfield continued, "I instantly cried out and chased the scoundrel. When I caught up with him, I managed to seize his collar and drag him back to the spot where the child still lay on the ground. A group of people had already gathered, including the girl's family and the doctor who had been called to the scene. The trampled child turned out to be more frightened than hurt, thank heavens, but the group of us was not about to let the stranger get away unpunished.

"There was something odd about our reactions to this man," Mr. Enfield remarked with a finger on his chin. "It is certainly natural to despise a man like this. But there was something else involved that I can't quite put my finger on. I had taken a dislike to him at first sight, even before the collision at the corner. And the doctor, usually in control of his emotions, looked like he was going to rip the stranger to shreds.

"Well, since killing him was out of the question, we did the next best thing. We told the man we would make a scandal out of the episode. He was beginning to look frightened as our group stood around him like vultures ready to attack. But he managed to keep a dark manner of coolness. He was smirking as if he knew something that could keep him out of trouble. I tell you my friend, I saw the devil in this man.

"To keep us from spreading the news, he offered up money," Mr. Enfield continued. " 'Name your figure,' he said. We told him we'd accept a hundred pounds for the child's family. He agreed and took us to this very place we are standing in front of right now. He whipped out a key to the door, went inside, and came back quickly with ten pounds in gold and a check for the rest. The check was signed with a well-known, honorable name—a name that I dare not mention.

"I wondered if the signature was real, or a phony likeness forged by the man, and I asked him as much. I explained that it was hardly believable that a man could walk into a cellar door at four in the morning and come out with another man's check for almost a hundred pounds. But without so much as a flinch, he insisted upon coming to the bank with me the next morning to cash the check himself. I was completely shocked to discover that the check was indeed genuine!"

Mr. Utterson's eyes and mouth were wide with shock. Mr. Enfield took notice and paused, letting his elder cousin absorb all that had just been told. This story was too much for Mr. Utterson's ears to bear! All of his senses seemed to go out of whack, and he had to take a deep breath before his cousin could continue.

"I see you feel as I do," said Mr. Enfield. "This is a horribly bizarre story. I've been going over and over again in my mind why a kind, well-respected member of society would be inclined to hand over a check to the devil in disguise. So far, the only explanation I have come up with is blackmail. An honest man paying through the nose for some of the mischievous mistakes of his youth. Blackmail House is what I call that place with the door now. Though even that, you know, is far from explaining all," he added.

"Does this well-respected check signer live behind this door?" asked Mr. Utterson.

"No, in fact, he doesn't," replied Mr. Enfield. "I noticed a different address for him on the front of the check. And I have studied the windowless structure for myself. It seems that no one other than the wicked gentleman goes in or out of that door, and only once in a great while. The chimney is usually smoking, so perhaps somebody does live there. But the buildings are so close to

each other that it's hard to say where one ends and another begins."

Mr. Utterson looked grief-stricken. "If you will, my good man," he dared to ask, "please tell me the name of the man who walked over the child."

"I suppose it can do no harm," replied Mr. Enfield. "Just please, let's keep this between ourselves, my friend."

The lawyer nodded solemnly and silently.

"It was a man by the name of Hyde," said his cousin.

Utterson was suddenly aware of a biting chill in the air and he shuddered. "What does he look like?" he asked.

"Hyde is difficult to describe," said Mr. Enfield. "There is something displeasing, something downright repulsive about this creature. But I simply cannot pinpoint one obvious deformity. What I can tell you is that there is something clearly not right about him."

"You are sure he used a key to enter

that door?" inquired Mr. Utterson in lawyer-like fashion.

"Have you any reason to doubt anything I have told you?" replied Mr. Enfield, surprised.

"I apologize," said Mr. Utterson. "It is just that right now I am hoping there has been some error in what you have just told me. If not, I am certain I know the name of the signer of the check."

Standing still and silent for a moment, Mr. Enfield went over the disturbing events he had just recounted. "I fear that I've been exact in every detail of my story, my esteemed cousin," he said.

Mr. Utterson sighed and the two agreed not to share the story with anyone else. The lawyer did not, however, reveal who it was he believed to have signed the check. Then the friends shook hands and parted as the sun disappeared below the horizon.

Chapter 2

DR. JEKYLL'S WILL

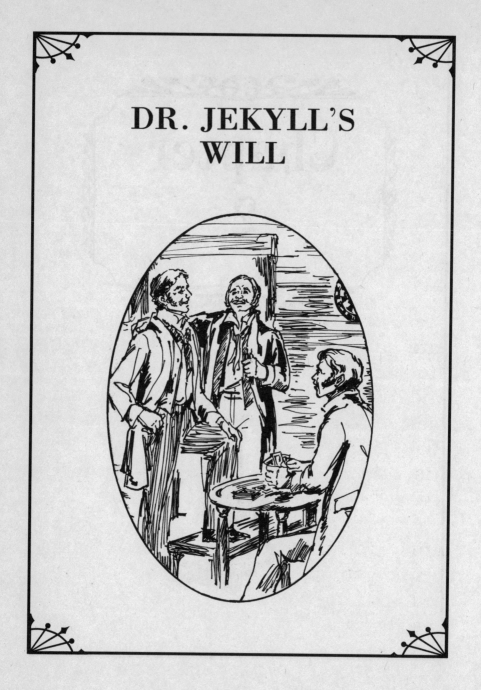

$\mathcal{M}$r. Utterson returned to his house and sat down to dinner. Although his stomach was empty, his mind was full, and he was unable to eat more than a few bites of pigeon pie. His restless mind then took him into his study. There he opened his safe and took from it an envelope marked *Dr. Jekyll's Will.*

The lawyer withdrew the document and examined its contents, more bewildered now than when it was first put in his charge. It plainly stated that in the case of Dr. Henry Jekyll's death, or in the case of his "disappearance or unexplained absence for a period longer than three months," all his possessions were to pass into the hands of his "friend and benefactor," Edward Hyde.

"I couldn't understand it before," Mr. Utterson pondered aloud, "what would lead an upstanding man like Jekyll to design such an odd will. But, in light of all I now know about this detestable devil called Hyde, I can only imagine that he knows of some disgraceful secret the good doctor wishes to cover up. And as I feared, I am sure Jekyll is the man who signed the check!"

With that, the lawyer returned the will to its safe, put on his coat, and set forth in the direction of Cavendish Square to visit the dependable Dr. Lanyon. "If anyone knows anything when it comes to Dr. Jekyll," thought Utterson, "it is our dear friend Lanyon."

Utterson was greeted by Lanyon's butler and quickly ushered into the dining room, where the esteemed doctor sat alone with an almost empty plate in front of him. At the sight of his visitor, the hearty, well-dressed gentleman sprang up from his chair and welcomed him joyfully with both hands. Utterson, Lanyon, and

Jekyll were old college friends.

After a little small talk, the lawyer eased into the uncomfortable subject he wished to bring up.

"I suppose, Lanyon," he said, "that you and I must be the two oldest friends that Henry Jekyll has?"

"Well, I wish his friends were younger," chuckled Dr. Lanyon. "But I suppose we have been his friends the longest. However, I haven't had the pleasure of the good doctor's company as of late. Is he well?"

"Oh, well yes, I suppose healthwise the doctor is fine," said Utterson, somewhat surprised. "But what's happened? I would think two scientists with common interests would spend a great deal of time together."

"Henry Jekyll has begun to have strange scientific notions about things," said Lanyon. "I believe he's gone wrong in mind, a little loopy if you know what I mean, although I take

an interest in him for old time's sake."

"Well, have you ever come across his friend—for lack of a better word—a man called Hyde?" asked Utterson.

"Hyde?" repeated Lanyon. "No. Never heard of him."

That was all the information the lawyer left with that evening, and he returned to his house with an uneasy mind. He tossed and turned in a fitful sleep, reliving his cousin's tale of terror over and over in his nightmares. And when the clock struck six o'clock the next morning, the lawyer awoke with a strong curiosity to see Mr. Hyde in person.

Chapter 3

HYDE AND SEEK

$\mathcal{F}$rom that day forward, whenever he was able, Mr. Utterson began to linger in the shops on the street of Blackmail House. He was waiting to get a good look at the man who had some kind of mysterious power over his unfortunate friend.

"We shall play a game of Hyde and Seek!" Utterson had thought to his own amusement.

At last his patience was rewarded. One chilly night at ten o'clock, after the shops had closed, the side street was empty and silent. Mr. Utterson had been leaning in a shop's doorway when he heard a quick, light footstep approaching. His heart leaped in his chest and instinctively he stepped out onto the street.

He quickly realized that he had just found the man he had been searching for. As the gentleman walked towards him, Utterson noted that he was small and plainly dressed. But, even from a distance, there was something about this

man's appearance which caused the lawyer to want to look away, although he did his best not to do so.

Then, suddenly, the small man crossed the street, headed for the battered door, and drew a key from his pocket. Before he could open the door, Mr. Utterson stepped out of the shadows and touched him on the shoulder.

"Mr. Hyde, I presume?" said Utterson.

Mr. Hyde shrunk back in fear, with a hissing intake of breath. He quickly pulled himself together and answered coolly, "That's my name. What do you want?"

"I see you are going in," replied the lawyer, staring directly into the fiend's face. "I am Mr. Utterson, an old friend of Dr. Jekyll's, and meeting you here so conveniently, I thought I might be able to go in with you."

"Dr. Jekyll is not in right now. He is away for awhile," hissed Hyde. And then he snapped, "How did you know my name?"

"By description," was the reply.

"Whose description?"

"We have common friends," said the lawyer.

"Who are they?" asked Mr. Hyde, his voice cracking slightly.

"Jekyll, for example."

"You're a liar! He never mentioned me!" cried Hyde, his neck flushing red with anger.

"Hush," said Mr. Utterson, "There is no need to get so riled, Mr. Hyde. I simply..."

The small man interrupted the lawyer with a harsh, sinister laugh that pierced the quiet night air like the howl of a wolf. And in the next moment, he swiftly unlocked the door and disappeared inside the house, slamming the door behind him.

The lawyer stood outside where Mr. Hyde had left him, trembling yet somehow satisfied at having seen the hideous Hyde at last. He began to walk down the street, pausing every step or two to think. Mr. Hyde was short in stature and pale in complexion. He seemed deformed somehow, but there were no clear markings.

And he had spoken with a husky, whispering voice. All of this was plain and true, but in itself could not explain the disgust and fear which Mr. Utterson felt towards him.

"Perhaps it is his wicked soul that comes to the surface," thought Mr. Utterson aloud. "Oh, my poor Henry Jekyll. I believe I have just met Satan in your new friend!"

The lawyer walked around the corner to a street lined with ancient houses, most of which were home to London's high society. One of the houses belonged to Dr. Henry Jekyll. Mr. Utterson knocked at the door and was greeted by Poole, Jekyll's well-dressed, elderly butler.

"Is Jekyll at home, Poole?" asked the lawyer.

"Please come in and have a seat while I check," answered Poole, leading Mr. Utterson into a large, comfortable den with a fireplace and a warm sofa. Then the butler left the room.

The lawyer began to get an uneasy feeling. He was usually received with a very warm welcome in this room. But tonight, the firelight cast strange shadows on the oak cabinets. There was also a chill in the air, despite the fire, which caused the lawyer to shudder. He was ashamed of his relief when Poole returned to say that Dr. Jekyll had gone out.

The lawyer could not help but ask, "Poole, is it okay for Mr. Hyde to go into that old building around the corner when Dr. Jekyll is away from home?"

"Oh, yes sir," replied the butler. "By Dr. Jekyll's orders, Mr. Hyde is allowed into the laboratory. He has a key."

"Very well then. Goodnight, Poole."

"Goodnight, Mr. Utterson."

The lawyer headed home with a heavy heart. "My poor old friend. We all have secrets from our past, some worse than others to be sure. But why do you deserve this type of punishment? This dreadful Hyde must have some dark secrets of his own, by the looks of him—secrets that I imagine are far worse than yours. I must find a way to expose the evil wretch and wreck his power over you. If he knows about the will he may grow impatient to inherit! Oh, dear Jekyll, if only you will let me help you...no time must be wasted, for I fear you are in grave danger!"

Chapter 4

THE PROMISE

As fortune would have it, Mr. Utterson soon received an invitation to Dr. Jekyll's home for a dinner party. He was anxious to confront the doctor about the will, so he made arrangements to remain behind after the other guests had departed. The doctor was pleased. After the effort of being the lively host, he found it comforting to sit with the quiet lawyer before being left alone for the rest of the evening.

But tonight, Dr. Jekyll's relaxation was disrupted by an unusually talkative lawyer.

"I've been wanting to speak to you about your will, Jekyll," began Mr. Utterson.

Quickly changing the subject, Jekyll said, "So I understand you had a visit with our dear friend Lanyon," and under his breath, "That foolish coward. Oh, I know he's a good fellow—you needn't frown. I just find it absurd that he should call himself a scientist. The zombie doesn't even experiment! He just accepts what he is given and what he is told...sorely disappointing indeed."

"You know I never approved of the will," Mr. Utterson said, ignoring the doctor and returning to the matter at hand.

"My will? Oh, yes, I know that," said the doctor, shifting uncomfortably in his easy chair.

"Well, I now know more about your Mr. Hyde and I feel it is my obligation to tell you how displeased I am," said Utterson.

The doctor's distinguished, handsome face grew pale and the light in his eyes vanished. "I would rather not discuss this with you, Utterson. You would not understand the difficult situation I am in and, believe me, there is nothing you can do to help it."

Utterson came back with, "I beg to differ, my good friend. You know I can be trusted and my resources are great."

"My friend, this is very good of you, and I cannot find the words to thank you. I do trust you completely. But believe me, this is an extremely private matter. Nevertheless, to put your mind at rest, I will assure you of one thing—the moment I choose to, I can be rid of Hyde. I give you my word on that."

"I apologize then, for overreacting," said the lawyer. "It seems that you have everything under control. Or, at the very least, you do a fine job of pretending all is well."

"Thank you, my good man," said the doctor, with an obvious sigh of relief. "I really do have a great interest in poor Hyde, and I only ask you to promise me one thing. If I should be taken away in some manner, please make sure the terms of my will are carried out. If you knew what I do, I think you would. And it would be a weight off my mind if you would make me this promise."

Utterson looked straight into Dr. Jekyll's dark, pleading eyes and saw a tortured soul. Although he knew he would later regret it, he finally said, "I promise."

Chapter 5

WITNESS
TO A CRIME

*A*lmost a year later, on a clear October night, London was startled by a horrifying crime against one of the most highly regarded men in town. The shocking scene was witnessed by a young woman who lived alone in a house not far from the river. She had been sitting by the window in her second-story bedroom, gazing dreamily at the brilliant full moon.

Suddenly, the woman was distracted out of her reverie by the sight of a nice-looking older gentleman with a shock of white hair. He was approaching a very small gentleman, to whom at first she paid less attention.

When the men passed right beneath the woman's window, she quickly recognized the small man as a certain Mr. Hyde. He had once visited her boss at work. She recalled feeling the same intense dislike for him then as she felt at this moment.

The old man must have been asking Mr. Hyde for directions, because he was pointing and writing something down. But Hyde appeared impatient, and suddenly began swinging his cane wildly about. Then, in a fit of rage, he began stamping his feet and carrying on like a madman. The old man stepped back and looked more than a little frightened.

The next moment, with ape-like fury, the cad struck the poor gentleman with his cane until he fell to the ground. Then Hyde trampled over his victim and ran away. At the horror of these sights and sounds, the woman fainted.

At two o'clock in the morning, the witness awoke and called the police.

When she went back to the window she saw the old man still lying in the street, and beside him part of the wooden cane which had been Hyde's weapon. When the police arrived they confirmed that the victim was dead, and they found a sealed and stamped envelope in his coat pocket—addressed to Mr. Utterson.

The next morning, the police brought the envelope to the lawyer, who was getting ready to go to work. They told him of the night's awful events. "We were hoping you could help us identify the victim and lead us to the culprit," said Inspector Newcomen.

"Yes, I recognize the poor soul," said Utterson when they arrived at the police station. "I am sorry to say that this is Sir Danvers Carew, the esteemed politician and a client of mine. The contents of the envelope pertain to legal matters he and I were to discuss."

The inspector presented the broken cane and said, "Perhaps you can help us find the man who committed this heinous crime."

At one look, broken and battered as it was, Utterson knew it was the cane he had given Henry Jekyll years before as a gift. He must have passed it on to his new friend Hyde.

"Yes," sighed the lawyer, suddenly

feeling queasy, "I think I can take you to the home of one Edward Hyde."

Utterson hailed a cab and gave the driver directions to a street located in Soho, a section of London which was home to crooks of all kinds. As they turned onto Bellview Lane, a great fog lifted, revealing a row of broken-down homes, once the manors and estates of the uppercrust.

A chill ran up the lawyer's spine as he stepped out of the cab onto the sidewalk. He knew that evil lurked in every nook and cranny of these seedy surroundings.

As they climbed the front steps to a large house with a rusted plaque above the door that read "The Churchills," they were greeted by a sour-faced old woman.

The woman eyed the two suited men suspiciously and squawked, "What do you want?" The lawyer asked her if a Mr. Hyde resided there. She said that although he did, he very rarely came home. In fact, until yesterday it had been almost two months since she'd seen him. And yesterday he was only home for about an hour.

"Well then, we wish to see his rooms," said the lawyer. And when the

woman began to protest he said, "Maybe you don't understand. This is Inspector Newcomen of Scotland Yard."

"Ah ha!" she shouted with shameless delight, "Hyde is in trouble! What has that miserable monster done now?"

The inspector and the lawyer exchanged knowing looks. "He is not a very popular character," said the inspector, "and we have come to find out why that is. And now, my good woman, please let us have a look about the place."

When they finally made it past the woman and entered one of Hyde's rooms, they were surprised to find it decorated in luxury and fine taste. In one corner stood a wine closet, on the walls hung expensive framed art, and oriental carpets covered the termite-infested floors. No doubt Hyde had weaseled away these riches from the good doctor.

But they also noticed that the dresser drawers were open and looked

as if they'd been ransacked. And in a small fireplace lay a pile of ashes, as though papers had been burned. From the ashes, the inspector pulled out the stub end of a checkbook.

Just as they were about to leave, Utterson saw the other half of the cane—the murder weapon—leaning against the door. This was all the proof they needed to connect Hyde to Carew's murder.

A visit to the bank inscribed on the charred checkbook revealed that there was a great deal of money still in Hyde's account. This gave the inspector new hope.

"Now we've got him!" he told Utterson. "Hyde obviously left in a panic, or he wouldn't have burned his checkbook and left the cane behind. He'll certainly need this money soon.

We shall give the bank a picture of Hyde and they will let us know when he comes to collect."

The inspector's perfect plan soon fell apart. No photos or family members of Hyde's could be found. And when an artist tried to draw Hyde from the descriptions of a few people, he was unable to provide a good likeness. Each person seemed to be describing someone different. The only thing they agreed upon was that Hyde seemed to be deformed somehow, although no one could be specific. And this was of no help to the artist.

Chapter
6

THE LETTER

*L*ater that afternoon, Utterson paid Dr. Jekyll a visit. He was greeted by Poole, who led him out the back door, and across a courtyard, to a building directly in back of the house. The lawyer recognized the dingy, windowless structure at once. This was where Hyde had gotten the tainted check! The lawyer hadn't realized until now that there was a back entrance to Dr. Jekyll's house.

As he made his way through a dark, tunnel-like hallway, he detected a dank, sickly smell and he winced. When he

came out into the lab, he saw that every inch of the tables was covered with brightly-colored, pungent chemicals in tubes and beakers. At the far end of the room was a flight of stairs.

Poole climbed the stairs, with the lawyer at his heels, and knocked on the

door to Jekyll's office.

"Mr. Utterson to see you, sir," called the butler through the closed door.

"It's open. Poole, please let my friend in," answered the doctor in a weary voice.

Here sat Dr. Jekyll by the fire, looking dreadfully ill. He did not rise to meet his visitor, but held out an ice-cold hand to bid him welcome. "I'm so glad you came," said the doctor in a strange, cracked voice.

As soon as Poole left them, Utterson said, "So, have you heard the news?"

The doctor shuddered. "I heard them crying it in the square," he said. "The murder has created quite a scandal, I suppose."

"You suppose? But of course!" remarked Utterson. "Listen, my cherished friend, I know this horrid Hyde character has some sort of stranglehold on you, but please assure me that you have not been mad enough to hide this creature!"

"Utterson, believe me, he does not want my help," cried the forlorn doctor. "He is gone, gone for good. Mark my words, he will never be heard from again."

"Well, Henry, for your sake, and for the safety of others, I hope you are right. But how can you be so certain?" asked the lawyer, highly doubtful.

"I am quite certain, although I cannot say why. Just please put your faith in me, as you have done so many times before," the doctor pleaded.

"Do you fear that your telling me the truth will lead to his detection?" asked the lawyer.

"No," said the doctor. "I don't care any longer what becomes of Hyde. I only wish to protect myself now. I do not want my good name smeared in connection with this man and his monstrous deeds. People will begin to think I have fallen from grace. And I cannot let that happen—I *will* not!" cried the doctor, shaking his fists in the air. Then suddenly, a coughing fit came on and Dr. Jekyll was gasping for air.

"Please, my good man," said Utterson, gently patting the doctor's back, "I beg of you, please calm down. I can see that all this stress has put a terrible strain on your health. Can I ask Poole to get you some hot tea?"

"No, thank you," replied the doctor, regaining his composure. "I will be just fine in good time, you will see. But there is one thing left to discuss with you, my friend. I have received a letter from Hyde, and don't know if I should show it to the police. I would like to leave it with you, Utterson, for I know you will get it into the right hands."

The lawyer took the letter and studied it carefully. It read:

Dear Dr. Jekyll,

How could I possibly repay you for your generosity? Certainly unworthy and undeserving of your kindness, I ask only that you do not worry about my safety. I have found a rather dependable means of escape. A thousand thanks are not enough.

Edward Hyde

The lawyer was very pleased with this letter. Although it didn't disclose Hyde's whereabouts, at least it shed some light on the bond between he and Jekyll. It was apparent that Hyde felt a debt of gratitude for Jekyll's overwhelming generosity. Utterson was surprised, yet relieved.

However, there was one more thing that continued to nag at the lawyer. "Jekyll, who dictated the terms of your will regarding the possibility of your 'disappearance'?"

The doctor seemed as if he were about to faint. The lawyer shook him to keep him from falling out of consciousness. "It was Hyde," Jekyll mumbled.

"Just as I thought," said Utterson. "He was planning to murder you! You have had quite a narrow escape."

"I have had a great deal more than an escape," said the doctor. "I have learned a very precious lesson." Then the doctor turned his face toward the fire, and Utterson thought he could see tears welling in the doctor's eyes.

The lawyer left as the doctor stared silently into the fire. Yet Jekyll seemed to be much more peaceful and content than when Utterson had first arrived. Utterson hoped that by taking the matter of Hyde's letter into his own hands it would ease the doctor's burden.

On his way out, Utterson stopped to speak with Poole. He said, "A letter was dropped off here today for Dr. Jekyll. Did you see the person who brought it?" But

Poole was sure nothing had come except by regular mail, "And nothing very interesting at that," he added.

This information gave the lawyer new insight. Obviously the letter had to have come by the laboratory door. If not, it had been written inside the doctor's office. Could Hyde have been there before he disappeared?

Utterson's first move was to contact his head law clerk, Mr. Guest, an expert on handwriting. "I have a document here, written by the murderer of Sir Danvers Carew. It is in his own handwriting."

Guest loved the challenge of a brand new case to crack. He sat down and studied the letter eagerly. "Well, the handwriting is definitely odd, but not one of a madman."

Just then, the servant entered with a note addressed to Mr. Utterson.

"Is that from Dr. Jekyll, sir?" asked the clerk. "I thought I recognized the handwriting. Is it private?"

"Only an invitation to his home for dinner. Why? Would you like to see it?"

"Yes, if I may," replied Guest. Then he laid the two sheets of paper alongside each other and stared at them for a few silent moments.

"Why are you comparing them, Guest?" Utterson finally asked.

"Well, sir," said the clerk, his eyes shining with the thrill of discovery, "the two hands are very similar, only differently sloped."

Mr. Utterson put his hand to his collar, for suddenly it seemed too tight and he felt as if he were choking. He loosened his tie and cleared his throat.

"I bid you not to speak of this to anyone," said Utterson to his clerk.

"I understand, sir," said Mr. Guest.

Alone later in his study, Mr. Utterson locked the note into his safe. "What the devil is going on here?" he thought, running a hand through his hair. "Henry Jekyll has forged a letter to protect a murderer!" And his blood ran cold in his veins.

Chapter 7

RAT FOOD

*T*he hunt for Hyde continued and thousands of pounds were offered in reward for his whereabouts. As the days passed, Mr. Utterson grew more deeply relieved that Hyde couldn't be found. Whatever grief he still felt over the death of Sir Danvers was somewhat soothed by the murderer's disappearance.

For Jekyll, the withdrawal of this evil influence from his life made all the difference. Soon he was out and about, his health greatly improved. For more than two months he seemed at peace.

During this time, Utterson was invited more than once to the doctor's home for dinner parties with the usual circle of friends, including Dr. Lanyon. It felt just like the old days—the sunny doctor displaying his customary charm and endless generosity. But in mid-January, on a spur-of-the-moment visit to Jekyll's, Utterson was refused entrance.

Rather disappointed by this unexpected treatment, he asked Poole for an explanation. "The doctor is confined to the house," said the butler, "and will see no one." Then he simply shut the door.

Three days later, the lawyer attempted another visit, only to have the door shut to him again. Feeling in need of companionship, he asked his clerk, Mr. Guest, to dine with him. The next night he went to Dr. Lanyon's.

There at least he was welcome, but when he came in, he was shocked at the change in his friend's appearance. The doctor had the ghostly look of a man who is about to die, or who fears that death is upon him! When the lawyer asked what had befallen the ill-looking doctor, Lanyon declared himself a doomed man.

"Well, life has been pleasant," he began. "I've liked it well enough. But now I have entered a state of shock from which I will never recover. I am only glad that I have avoided this kind of torture for this long. Now, I am ready to surrender to it."

"Lanyon! Get a grip, my good man!" exclaimed Utterson. "Jekyll is ill, too. Have you seen him? I haven't been able to make it past the front door."

Then Lanyon's eyes turned dark and he shuddered. "I wish to see or hear no more of Dr. Jekyll," he said in a hoarse voice. "I am finished with that person. I regard him as dead."

Utterson opened his mouth, but no words came out. He didn't know what to say or do next.

Lanyon put an end to the silence. "After I am dead, I hope you find out the truth. If you wish to stay and discuss another topic, please do. If not, please go, for I cannot bear it."

When he got home, Utterson wrote a letter to Dr. Jekyll:

My honorable and cherished friend,
Why do I arrive at your door only to have it shut in my face? How did I, of all people, suddenly become unworthy of your friendship? Not to mention the

good Dr. Lanyon. We are probably the best friends you will ever have in your lifetime. Perhaps our 'cheese sandwich' can remain intact as we planned, rather than each separate piece becoming food for lab rats in the end. Only the three of us can know what that means—surely that must tell you something. I plead for a speedy, forthright reply and the opportunity to remain...

Truly cheese between two pieces of bread,

Gabriel John Utterson, Esq.

The next day brought a long and unusually solemn reply:

Dear solitary cheese,

I fear we have all been exposed and it is too late to go back to being a 'sandwich.' We just may be food for the rats now. I cannot tell you how sorry I am. I share Lanyon's view that we must never meet. I wish to lead the rest of my life alone, as a plain 'slice of bread,' lacking substance. My layers have been stripped, and I cannot bear to be seen.

I have sinned and now I suffer in the darkest way. I am sure I deserve this, but my dear old friends do not. Utterson, I wish I could tell you more, but it is better to remain silent. Please respect that. I now remain...

Truly alone,

Dr. Henry E. Jekyll

Utterson was amazed beyond belief. These great changes in both Jekyll and Lanyon were somehow connected. But how? The lawyer was unsure if he would ever know.

Two weeks later, Dr. Lanyon died in his sleep. The night after his funeral, Utterson went into his study and locked the door. Sitting by the light of a lone candle, he took out of his coat pocket an envelope that read: *"PRIVATE: for the hands of G.J. Utterson alone. If he dies before opening this, it is to be destroyed unread."* It was in the handwriting of the dead doctor.

Taking a deep breath, the lawyer opened the envelope, only to find an inner envelope marked as follows: *"Not to be opened until the death or disappearance of Dr. Henry Jekyll."* He did not believe his eyes.

Pacing back and forth between his desk and the vault, he considered ripping the envelope open. But professional honor and faith to his departed friend stopped him. The envelope stayed sealed in the corner of his private safe.

His restlessness and curiosity increasing over the following days, the lawyer found himself at Jekyll's doorstep time and again. Oddly, he was more satisfied with the daily reports from Poole than if he had actually been shown into the house of hidden horrors.

Poole, however, did not have very pleasant news to impart to the unwanted guest. The doctor had begun to confine himself to the office over his laboratory. He never requested anyone's company or even read a book.

Chapter
8

A REMARKABLE CHANGE

*I*t just so happened that on one of the usual Sunday walks taken by Mr. Utterson and his cousin, Mr. Enfield, they somehow ended up on the same street where each had first seen Edward Hyde.

"Thank goodness Hyde is gone forever," said Enfield.

"I hope you're right," said Utterson. "I am worried about Jekyll. Let's step into the courtyard. Even if we can't go inside, perhaps we can get his attention through the office window and visit with him that way."

"I didn't know this was connected to Jekyll's home," declared Enfield as they entered the courtyard.

"Yes, indeed, I just found out recently myself," said Utterson just as the sun began to set. "Oh, look, there he is!"

Sitting beside a window, about halfway open, was Dr. Jekyll. He looked out with a blank stare like a man who is confined to a prison cell. Then his eye caught Utterson's and he quickly began to shut the window.

"What?! Hey, Jekyll!" the lawyer cried out, "Wait! How are you feeling?"

Jekyll hesitated, then opened the window again and held out his hand to prevent the two men from coming any closer. They had to squint their eyes to focus on the doctor. He looked pale and...different somehow.

"I am not well, Utterson," said Jekyll. "It will not last long, though, thank goodness."

"You stay indoors too much," said Utterson. "This is Mr. Enfield. Would you care to join us for some fresh air?"

"Thank you for thinking of me. However, I cannot...I dare not."

"Very well then, old friend, we'll just stay put and talk to you from right here."

"I would like that very much," said the doctor. But when the two men began to come closer, without warning, Jekyll slammed the window shut and disappeared.

Not until Utterson and Enfield reached the bustling center of town did they utter a single word to one another. And, when Utterson finally turned to look at his companion, he saw the same horror in his cousin's eyes that he himself felt.

"We never should have gone there," said Utterson. Mr. Enfield only nodded his head in agreement, and they walked on in silence once more.

Chapter
9

A CHILLING
DISCOVERY

*O*ne evening after dinner, Mr. Utterson was quite surprised to receive a visit from Poole.

From the butler's anxious expression, the lawyer gathered that he bore a heavy weight he wished to unload. "What brings you here that burdens you so, Poole?"

"You know how the doctor shuts himself up in that cramped office, sir. Well, he's shut up again in there and I just don't like the looks of things, sir, and..."

"Yes, Poole, what is it?" asked Utterson, growing impatient.

"It's just that I'm afraid, sir, and I can bear it no longer," Poole replied, without mentioning exactly what frightened him.

"Please," begged the lawyer, trying desperately to avoid hollering at him for coming over in such a state and then shutting up like a clam. "Just relax, Poole. I can see that something is upsetting you, and it must be very serious. Please just tell me what it is."

"Well, sir, you see..." he paused, then said rapidly, "I think there has been foul play."

"Foul play!" cried the lawyer, jumping out of his seat and raising his voice. "What are you saying?"

"I dare not say, sir," said Poole, even more distressed at seeing the lawyer in such agony. "Well, why don't you come with me and see for yourself."

It was a cold, windy March night. The wispy clouds overhead flew by in a fury as if they were whipping up a great storm. Mr. Utterson pulled his coat snugly around his shivering body and followed Poole, who kept a pace or two ahead. The streets they crossed were totally empty.

After what seemed like ages, they reached Dr. Jekyll's front door. Poole knocked in a series of three short raps.

"Is that you Poole?" asked a whispering voice from within.

"Yes, it's all right. Let us in," said Poole. They entered to find all of the doctor's servants huddled around the fireplace in the hallway.

"What on earth is going on here?" asked the lawyer.

"They are all afraid," said Poole.

"Of what?"

"Please, follow me, sir," said Poole as he led the way by the light of a lamp, the flame of which flickered in the icy wind.

Utterson shivered and suddenly had the feeling he should run the other way without looking back. But his feet continued to follow Poole. Finally, they arrived at the door to the doctor's office. Turning to face Utterson, the light from the lamp cast an eerie glow on the butler's pale face.

"Now, sir," he said, "If for some reason the doctor asks you in, don't go."

Utterson's nerves were completely on edge. The muscles in his legs twitched. He would have lost his balance if Poole hadn't grabbed his arm at just the right moment.

"Please, sir, whatever you do, just

try to stay calm," said Poole, before taking his own deep breath of air. Then he knocked on the door and motioned for the lawyer to press his ear against it.

"Mr. Utterson is here, sir, asking to see you," Poole called out.

A voice answered from within, "Tell him I cannot see anyone."

Poole said nothing, and taking up his lamp, led Mr. Utterson back across the yard and into the doctor's kitchen. "Sir," he said, "you have now heard it as well as I. That is not the doctor's voice! It has been replaced by a low, gritty-sounding one."

Feeling lightheaded, Utterson quickly took a nearby seat. "Well, perhaps poor Jekyll is extremely ill, causing his voice to take on a new tone."

"No, sir. I have lived here twenty years. I know his voice well. I'm afraid the doctor's been done away with! Eight days ago the other servants and I heard him cry out in sheer terror. Whoever is responsible for the good doctor's murder is now locked in that office!"

"That sounds like a rather wild explanation, Poole," said Utterson. "Suppose it were true, then why would the murderer stay? It just doesn't make sense."

"I believe I can prove it to you," answered Poole. "For the past eight days, whatever, or whomever, lives in that office has been crying, night and day, begging for some sort of medicine. The doctor used to write his requests on a sheet of paper and leave it on the stairs for me. Well, this week there have been two or three sheets of paper each day requesting the same drug. Every time I bring the stuff back, there is another paper telling me to return it, because it is not pure. This drug is wanted very badly, sir, though I wish I knew what for."

"Do you have any of these papers?" asked Mr. Utterson.

Poole took a crumpled note out of his pocket and handed it to the lawyer:

Sirs, Dr. Jekyll has found your last sample to be impure. In the year 18—, Dr. Jekyll purchased some of pure quality from your firm. Should any of the same be left, please forward it to him at once. Money is no object. For heaven's sake, find some of the old brew!"

"This is a strange note," said Utterson. "All at once at the very end comes an outburst of raging emotion. Why do you still have this note if it was supposed to be given to the chemist?"

"The man at Maw's was very angry and insulted, sir. He threw it back to me like so much dirt," replied Poole.

"I still don't understand why you think the doctor has been murdered. This appears to be in his handwriting."

"What does it matter if it looks like the doctor's handwriting," said Poole in a testy manner. "I have seen the creature who stays in Jekyll's office!"

"You've seen him? Well, go on my good man!" cried Utterson, beginning his trademark pace back and forth.

"It happened this way," began Poole. "I had come into the laboratory for my nightly call. It seems he had come out of the office to look for this drug. There he was at the far end of the room digging among the crates. When he saw me he gave a sharp yelp like a wounded animal. Then he whipped upstairs into the office.

It was only for a minute that I saw him, but my hair stood on end and goosebumps covered my skin. I know it was not the doctor simply wearing a mask because this creature was also dwarfish. The good doctor was a tall man with a fine build. I believe in my heart that a murder was committed."

"We both know who this man is, don't we Poole?" Utterson remarked.

"Yes, sir. I saw him very quickly, but I think it was Mr. Hyde. I could tell by the chill I felt in my bones. Who else could have gotten in by the laboratory door?"

"Indeed! I believe you," said Mr. Utterson. "I believe poor Jekyll has been

killed, and that his murderer still lurks in the victim's office—although I cannot figure out why. And now, I consider it my duty to break in that door."

"Ah! Very well then!" cried Poole with much relief. "I will help you." He picked up an ax, then asked two other servants to take their posts by the laboratory door.

When the lawyer and the butler arrived once more at the office door, they could hear footsteps inside. The steps fell lightly and slowly, different from the doctor's fast, heavy tread.

"Is there ever any other noise?" asked Mr. Utterson.

"Once I heard it weeping like a lost soul. I could've wept myself after hearing it," answered Poole.

Utterson gathered up his courage and then cried out in a loud voice, "Jekyll! I demand to see you." No reply. "If you don't let me in, I will be forced to break down this door. Our suspicions are aroused by your unusual habits."

"Utterson," said the gruff voice, "Please, have mercy!"

"That is not the voice of Jekyll—it is Hyde's!" cried Utterson. "Down with the door, Poole!"

The butler swung the ax at the wooden door with all his might. The building shook, but the door remained intact. A screech rang out from the office. Up went the ax again, but the wood was strong. It was not until the fifth blow that the lock burst and the door flew open.

The intruders, stunned by the stillness that followed their commotion, stood back and peered inside. A fire was burning in the hearth, papers sat neatly on the desk, and on the table sat a kettle and teacup.

In the middle of the room lay a twitching body. Drawing on his courage, Utterson rolled the body over. He was staring at Hyde's ghastly face.

Cold beads of sweat formed on the lawyer's forehead as he felt for a pulse, and finally confirmed that the treacherous Hyde was dead.

"He holds an empty tube in his hand. He must have swallowed a dangerous chemical," said Utterson. "We have come too late to save or to punish him. Now all that is left for us is to find the body of Dr. Jekyll."

"He must be buried in this building somewhere," said Poole. The pair scoured the laboratory, but there was no trace of Henry Jekyll, dead or alive. "Let's go back to the office and check there again."

They climbed the stairs in silence, and proceeded to examine the contents of the office. On one table were traces of a chemical experiment, mounds of some type of white powder laid out on glass saucers.

"That is the same drug I had been bringing him," said Poole. As he spoke, the kettle gave a startling whistle. This brought them over near the desk, where a large envelope sat on top of all the papers, bearing the name of Mr. Utterson. It was written in the doctor's handwriting. The lawyer unsealed it, and took out a will just like the one in his safe at home. All of the terms were the same, but in place of Edward Hyde's name as inheritor was the name Gabriel John Utterson!

"I am shocked," he said. "Hyde has had this document in his possession and hasn't destroyed it! He must have raged to see himself betrayed by the doctor. I just don't understand."

He noticed a letter with the will. It was written in the doctor's handwriting with the day's date at the top. "Oh, Poole!" the lawyer cried, "Jekyll was alive and here today! He could not have been killed and disposed of in such a short amount of time. He must have fled! But how?"

"Why don't you read the note, sir?" asked Poole.

My dear Utterson,

When you read this, I shall have disappeared, although under what circumstances I cannot know. But my instinct tells me that the end is sure and near. Please read Lanyon's report, which he warned me he would give to you. And then, if you care to hear more, turn to the confession of

Your unworthy and unhappy friend,
Henry Jekyll

"There's more in the envelope?" asked Utterson.

"Here it is, sir," said Poole, handing him a weighty packet.

The lawyer put it in his coat pocket. "Say nothing to anyone about this, Poole. Whatever has become of the doctor, we must protect his good name. I'm off for home to read these documents in quiet, but I shall be back before midnight. Then, and only then, we shall call for the police."

They left the building, locking the door of the laboratory behind them. Utterson trudged back to his house with the weight of ten thousand bricks upon his head.

Confronted by the answers to this dreadful investigation, the lawyer suddenly realized he was afraid to find out the truth. Still, in many ways, he was anxious to uncover this mystery once and for all.

Chapter 10

DR. LANYON'S REPORT

*H*eaving a great sigh, Mr. Utterson sat in his easy chair by the fire and enjoyed the quiet stillness that surrounded him. He could use a minute to calm his nerves and collect his thoughts before examining the documents that would change his life forever. Suddenly, there was a strange flicker from the fireplace and he saw shadows move across the wall. He quickly glanced over his shoulder towards the study door, but saw no one. Then he heard a slow, sad whistle which jerked him right out of his chair.

"Oh, I'm afraid my nerves are completely shot. The wind is simply whistling its way through the open window. I must go and shut it before I give in to my ridiculous fright."

After he shut the window, he thought he heard a soft, cackling laughter coming from...where? The chimney! He stepped over to the fireplace, but all he could hear was the crackling logs as they burned.

'No more of this nonsense. I must keep my head if I'm going to get through these papers tonight,' thought the lawyer. He sat down and withdrew Dr. Lanyon's document:

Four days ago, I received a letter addressed to me in the handwriting of my colleague and old school chum, Henry Jekyll. I was very surprised, since I had dined with him the night before, and he hadn't mentioned anything deserving of such formality.

His letter stated that he wished my help and stressed the dire importance of the matter. He went as far as to say that his life, honor, and reason were all at my mercy. If I failed him, he swore he would be lost. He asked me to postpone all my other engagements for that night. He instructed me to drive to his house, where Poole had been given orders to let me in. Then, I was to break into his office—by force if necessary. The contents of one particular drawer were to be brought back to my own home. The drawer was said to contain some powders, a vial, and a notebook.

Furthermore, I was told to make sure I was back at my house well before midnight. When the clock struck twelve, a stranger would arrive at my doorstep. I was to let him in and give him the contents of the drawer. This was all I had to do to win the good doctor's favor.

I received no explanation, just a tug at my heart strings—"By the neglect of one of these tasks, you may have charged your conscience with my death or the wreck of my reason."

You can see how I felt bound to do as he requested. The less I understood of this mess, the less I was in a position to judge its importance. I simply took my old friend's word and set upon the deeds at hand.

Wasting no time, I hopped into a hansom cab and drove straight to Jekyll's house. I was greeted by Poole, who had been given instructions identical to mine. He had already sent for a locksmith and a carpenter. They had been attempting for almost an hour by now to enter the locked office door without causing much damage. Finally, after one more hour, the locksmith was successful and the door stood open.

My eyes darted around the room, stopping every now and then to record a broken flask, torn pages from a book. I thought perhaps I could come up with my own answers to this bizarre situation. It turned out, however, that I left with the drawer and its contents more baffled than I came.

When I returned to Cavendish Square, I examined the items closely. The powders were in unmarked containers, so it was clear that they had been mixed by Jekyll, not given to him in this condition by the chemist. The vial was about half full of a blood-red liquid, which had a strong, bitter smell. I could not identify the substance. The notebook contained nothing but a series of dates. These covered a period of many years, but I noticed that the entries stopped nearly a year ago. The only words I found were next to a date recorded very early in the list—"Total Failure!!!" All I could make of this was that Jekyll had been keeping a record of a series of experiments.

I couldn't understand how my having these things would affect the honor, sanity, or life of my scatterbrained colleague. I began to think the poor doctor had acquired a disease of the brain and perhaps he was dangerous. I wondered if I would be in need of some measure of self-defense when this stranger arrived, so I loaded an old revolver.

The clock had barely struck midnight when I heard a soft knocking at the door. The noise startled me and I gasped. But I went to the door at once.

Before opening it I asked, "Are you the man sent here by Dr. Jekyll?"

"Yes, yes" he whispered urgently, bidding me to let him in. When I opened the door, he quickly entered and shut the door behind him.

As I followed him into the brightly lit den, I kept my hand on my weapon—just in case. Here, I finally had the chance to see him clearly, although once I did I was anxious to dim the lights. He was small but muscular, and wore a distasteful grimace on his face. I could not find a concrete reason for the loathing which I felt towards him.

This creature was dressed in a laughable fashion. His clothes, although they were expensive and well-made, were enormous on him—the pant legs of his trousers were rolled up to keep them from dragging on the ground, and his collar sprawled wide upon his shoulders. But I did anything but laugh.

In fact, I was revolted. This unfit attire simply emphasized his freakish qualities. And it peaked my curiosity even further as to his status in the world, his fortune, and where on earth he came from.

"Have you got the stuff?" he cried.

So impatient was he that he grabbed my arm and began to shake me.

I pried his fingers off me, conscious of an icy pang in my blood at his touch. I showed him to a comfortable seat and sat down in my own easy chair. It took a great effort to appear at ease, due to the lateness of the hour, my anxiety, and the horror I felt towards my visitor. But I gave it my best effort.

"Come, sir," I said. "You forget I have

not yet had the opportunity to get to know you."

"I beg your pardon," he replied in a strained, but polite manner. "My impatience has overcome my politeness. I apologize, but I...." He paused and put his hand to his throat. I could see, in spite of his collected manner, that he was trying to hold back the stirrings of a hysterical outburst. "The drawer!" he growled, "Please, sir, if you will."

I took pity on my visitor, and some perhaps on my own growing curiosity.

"There it is, sir," I said, pointing to the drawer on the floor, still covered with a sheet.

The animal sprung to it. I could hear him grunting and his teeth grating. His eyes bulged out of his head and he began to foam at the mouth! I grew alarmed both for his life and his reason.

"Compose yourself," I said as he pulled off the sheet.

At the sight of the contents, he uttered a loud sob of relief. "Do you have a measuring cup?" he asked, trying to maintain self-control.

I rose from my seat nervously and gave him what he asked for.

He nodded in thanks and measured out some of the red liquid in the cup, then added one of the powders. At first, the mixture was of a reddish hue, but as the crystals melted it began to brighten in color, to bubble, and to throw off vapor. Suddenly, the bubbling ceased and the concoction turned a dark purple, which then faded to a watery green. My visitor watched these changes with a sharp eye. He then smiled, set the cup down on the table, and turned to me.

"Now, will you be satisfied if I exit your door with this cup in hand, or has your curiosity gotten too much command of you? Think before you answer," he warned, "For it shall be done as you decide. If you choose to witness what comes next, you will behold scientific knowledge like none you had thought existed. And here, in this room, new avenues to fame and power will be open to you as they have been for me."

"Sir," I said, trying to appear calm, "I do not know what you speak of, but I have gone too far in this situation—with no explanations mind you—to miss the chance to see the end."

"And so you shall," replied my visitor. "Lanyon, remember your vows. What follows is strictly confidential, under the seal of our profession. And now, you who have so long been bound to the most narrow views of science, you who have denied the endless possibilities of medicine, you who have looked down upon your colleagues—behold!"

He put the cup to his lips, drinking the brew in one gulp. An animal cry followed. He staggered backward and clutched onto the table to keep from falling. Staring straight at me with glazed-over eyes and a gasping mouth, his face suddenly turned black. His features seemed to melt and rearrange. His body seemed to swell. I could not watch any longer. I lifted my arm to shield my eyes.

Suddenly, the noises stopped and there was silence. I peered out from behind my arm and almost fainted at what I saw before me. There before my eyes, pale and shaking like a man back from death, stood Henry Jekyll!

What he told me in the next hour as I sat in a state of shock I cannot bear to write down.

I saw what I saw, I heard what I heard, yet now I ask myself if I believe it. I cannot answer. My soul is sick with shock and grief. I don't know what is real and what isn't—my reason has left me. I feel that my days are numbered.

I must tell you one more thing, Utterson, if you can bring yourself to believe it. The creature who crept into my house that night was, by Jekyll's own confession, known by the name of Edward Hyde.

And now I bid you...goodbye.
HASTIE LANYON

Chapter
11

A SHOCKING
CONFESSION

*T*aking a deep breath, Mr. Utterson looked up at the hearth, where a lively fire was burning. Just as he was about to turn to Henry Jekyll's confession, he thought he saw two faces staring back at him from the flames. He got up from his chair and walked over to the fireplace, oddly feeling no fear. When he bent down to get a closer look, a voice surrounded him, as if it were coming from everywhere. He saw the faces of Dr. Jekyll and Mr. Hyde in the fire.

"Don't be frightened," the voice said. "We are one, Mr. Hyde and I. I am his good, while he is my evil."

It was Jekyll's voice! Or was it Hyde's? "What is that supposed to mean?" the lawyer asked the flickering flames.

"It means that both good and evil live in all of us," said the voice. "One cannot exist without the other. I found a way to bring out my evil side, and I thought I could do so without harming my good side. That, I have learned, is not possible.

"But the valuable lesson I wish to pass on to you, dear friend, is this—do not attempt to adjust your true nature. For the balance that must be struck between good and evil is born within you. That was my mistake. I thought I held the power to put one above the other whenever I wished. I know now that I was wrong."

Then the two faces faded from the fire, and Utterson was left staring into ordinary orange flames. After awhile, he recovered and went back to his desk, sat down, and slowly opened Henry Jekyll's confession:

I was born in the year 18— to a large fortune. My family taught me to respect the wise and the good among my fellow men. Indeed, the worst of my faults was a certain careless spirit of the heart. In its way it has made many people happy, but it has also caused in me great difficulty. As a scientist, I wished to be taken quite seriously by the academic world.

It quickly came about that I began to hide my youthful activities, which I worried some might consider childish and irresponsible. Another man may have boasted about such antics. But with the high standards I set for myself, I judged myself harshly. It was more these strict standards and less any real wrongdoing on my part that filled me with such guilt and shame.

It was this nagging sense of self-doubt that divided my one nature into two separate parts: good and ill. I began leading a double life. But I was as much myself when I plunged into shameful deeds as I was when I worked hard to relieve people's sorrow and suffering.

Therefore, it is not surprising that my scientific studies eventually led me to discover the truth—that man is not truly one, but two. And it is that knowledge that can make all the difference.

Even before my studies on the dual nature of man began, I used to daydream about the possibility of separating the elements of good and evil. For in one person, there is a constant struggle between these two forces. If the two could be placed in separate identities, each would be able to thrive without the other one threatening it. That's what I told myself, anyway.

As I started thinking about it more and more, I began to experiment. I mixed drugs day and night to find a combination that had the power to alter a person's identity—the ultimate challenge. Finally, I found the last ingredient and purchased a large quantity. Late one fateful night, I mixed the elements, watched them boil and smoke in the glass, and with a healthy dose of courage, drank the potion.

All at once my body trembled and I felt agony like never before. Then suddenly I felt myself again, as if coming out of a terrible illness. But there was something strange and new in my sensations. I felt younger, lighter, and healthier. I felt reckless and irresponsible. And I knew immediately that I had turned wicked.

Instantly, I became aware that I had shrunk in height. But there was no mirror in my office. So, determined

as I was to see myself, I decided to sneak to my bedroom. At this late hour I would go unnoticed while everyone slept. As I crossed the yard, I thought with wonder that I must be the first creature of this sort to be seen by the unsleeping stars. It gave me a delicious thrill. I stole through the corridors, and when I entered my room I saw Edward Hyde for the first time.

Speaking by theory alone, I suppose that the evil side of my nature, now at the forefront, was less strong than the good. After all, I had up till now led a life of mostly good deeds and self-control. The evil side had been much less active.

I believe that is why Edward Hyde was so much smaller, thinner, and younger than Henry Jekyll. But evil had made the face and body of Hyde seem hideous and deformed. And yet, when I looked into the mirror, I saw a welcome sight, not a repulsive one. For this, too, was myself. To me, it seemed natural and human, a livelier image of the spirit.

As Hyde, none could come near me without wincing or displaying some obvious sign of discomfort. This was most likely because Hyde, alone in the ranks of mankind, was pure evil. Others did not wish to see it, for if they did, perhaps they would see the evil in themselves.

I lingered only a moment at the mirror, for the second experiment was necessary to see if I had lost my identity as Dr. Jekyll completely. If so, I had to flee from this house that was no longer my own. Hurrying back to my office, I once more prepared and drank the potion. I suffered the same challenge of change and came to myself again, this time with the character, the height, and the mask of Henry Jekyll.

It was done! I had succeeded in separating good and evil. But wait...Jekyll was not *only* good as Hyde was only evil. Jekyll had been the one tormented by the struggle of the two forces. Both still remained in him. I realized that instead of creating separate homes for good and evil, I had unleashed the monster, while forsaking the angel.

Regardless of my newfound awareness and feelings of guilt, I had not yet learned my lesson. Due mostly to my new tempting power, I felt the urge to drink the potion over and over. During this time, I took and furnished a house in Soho for Mr. Hyde.

As Jekyll, I announced to my servants that a Mr. Hyde was to have full liberty and power about my house. I made sure to visit the house as Hyde on several occasions in the weeks that followed. I next drew up that will to which you objected, so that if anything should happen to Henry Jekyll I could still keep my possessions as Edward Hyde.

Finally, I felt prepared to lead my double life. Many people hire others to do their dirty work. I could use my alter ego and perform the dastardly deeds myself, unrecognized by the public eye. For it was me, but it wasn't me! One moment I could be standing tall with a wave of respect washing over me. The next, I could plunge headfirst into a sea of recklessness. And best of all, Dr. Jekyll's good name would remain unharmed.

The pleasures I originally intended to seek in my disguise were no doubt undignified, yet I wouldn't call them harmful. However, in the hands of Edward Hyde they began to turn monstrous. When I returned as Dr. Jekyll from the dark abyss of these jaunts, I was often choked by regret and remorse.

Still, I was at the mercy of the monster. His every act and thought centered on himself. Henry Jekyll was eventually able to soothe his conscience somewhat—after all, it was not he that was guilty of these sins. And by trying to undo the evil done by Hyde, he was able to put his mind even more at ease.

Although I'm sure you are bursting at the seams to know just what type of treachery Hyde was involved

in, I can think of no good reason to tell you much more than you already know. For why should I let you think any worse of me than you already must?

Believe it or not, I am still the man— the one and the same—that is your familiar friend. In fact, you probably know more about me than you care to admit to yourself, even things that I dare not write down here. For you, Gabriel John Utterson, know me better than anyone else. So perhaps you are not as shocked as you may feel. Think about it, look inside yourself, and you shall surely see. Therefore, I will spare you the gory details and continue to describe the events that led to my final transformation.

Chapter 12

THE LESSER OF TWO EVILS

About two months before the murder of Sir Danvers, I had been out for one of Hyde's adventures and returned at a late hour. Immediately, I swallowed the potion and went to sleep as Henry Jekyll. The next day, I woke feeling an odd sensation.

Squinting, I could see the fancy furniture and high ceilings of my room. However, something felt wrong, like I was not actually where I seemed to be—in Dr. Jekyll's room. I felt as if I were in the little room in Soho where I was accustomed to sleeping as Hyde.

Still rousing from a dream state, my eyes remained closed and I began to lazily question my confusion. It occurred to me that I was beginning to have difficulty remembering who I had last been. This thought caused me to chuckle. How silly! Of course, I had gone to sleep as Jekyll the night before, in the house in the grand square. My eyes then unglued and focused upon my hand.

Now, you know the hand of Henry Jekyll as large and firm, with well-manicured fingernails. Well, the hand which I now saw lying on the bedspread was lean, corded with veins, and had jagged, yellow fingernails. Needless to say, I was now wide awake, bolt upright where I lay. It was the hand of Edward Hyde.

I must have stared at it for five straight minutes. Stuck as I was in a numb stupor, I felt as if cymbals were crashing in my head. Finally bounding from my bed, I rushed to the mirror. At the sight of Hyde, my blood went icy and I trembled from head to toe.

Yes, I had gone to bed Henry Jekyll and awakened as Edward Hyde, without so much as a drop of the elixir!

How was this to be explained? How was it to be remedied? It was about ten o'clock in the morning, so all of the servants were up and about. All my drugs were in the office—a long journey down two pairs of stairs, through the back passage, across the courtyard and through the laboratory! It might indeed be possible to cover my face, but how would that help when I was unable to conceal my smaller size?

Before I really began to panic, an incredible sweet relief poured over me. I realized that the servants were already used to visits by my second self. I quickly dressed in clothes of my own size and had no sooner opened the bedroom door when I collided with Randi, the scullery maid, in the hall. She gawked and gasped at seeing Mr.

Hyde at such an odd hour of the day—
and coming out of the doctor's room! I
bolted right past her and managed to
avoid the others. Ten minutes later,
Dr. Jekyll returned and sat down to
breakfast in the kitchen.

Small indeed was my appetite, yet I
forced myself to sip some tea and eat
half a crumpet, sitting among the four

on my dish. Used to watching me devour all of his homemade treats each morning, the cook knew something was not quite right. He brought me a cold, wet towel when he noticed my perspiring brow and inquired if I was ill. I managed to mutter, "Thank you, Eric," then excused myself and retired to my office.

Here I sat and began to reflect more seriously than ever before on the complications of my double existence. It seemed as though lately the body of Edward Hyde had grown. Perhaps it was due to the increasing strength of his character. He was taking over, and Jekyll was slowly losing the voluntary power to make Hyde come and go.

I thought back to my early research. Once, very early in my experiments, the drug had totally failed me. Since then, on more than one occasion, I had doubled and sometimes tripled the dose! But then, I was having trouble changing from doctor to devil. Now it appeared I would need even greater doses to do the reverse. All things considered, it was clear that my original and better self was slipping away in favor of my dark creation.

Between Jekyll and Hyde I now felt I had to choose. For I was certain that if I did not take the matter into my hands while I still was able, Hyde would not give me the chance. I thought about what each had to offer. Both had memory in common, but all other aspects were unevenly shared between them. The doctor, kind and decent in many ways, still shared in the pleasures and adventures of his evil counterpart. After all, Jekyll was the original designer of the schemes set out for Hyde to act upon. But Hyde was indifferent to his creator, remembering him only as the outlaw remembers the shelter which shields him from pursuit.

To surrender Hyde and live as Jekyll was to lay my devilish appetite to rest. I would surely suffer without it. To destroy Jekyll and live as Hyde was to kill a thousand hopes and dreams, and to become forever despised and friendless. There was also another consideration. While Jekyll would suffer greatly for what he had lost, Hyde would not even care that he had given up his better half.

After tossing the choices back and forth in my mind, I chose the better part and prayed for the strength to keep to it. It's true, I preferred the elderly and discontented doctor, surrounded by friends and cherishing honest hopes. I said good-bye to the liberty, the youth and energy, and the secret pleasures...a final farewell to Edward Hyde. Still, I didn't give up the house in Soho, nor did I destroy Hyde's clothes. I cannot explain why.

For two months, I held myself to strict standards like never before. My conscience approved, and for that I was entirely grateful. But it didn't last long. I began to grow impatient with bittersweet longings, as if Hyde were struggling for freedom. At last, in an hour of moral weakness, I once again mixed and swallowed the cursed concoction.

Yet I was unprepared for what followed. I didn't realize that, in effect, I had caged an animal and was now letting him loose. The moment I drank the potion I felt a storm brewing in my soul...and Hyde came out roaring! He was furious and raging with a wicked hunger, much greater than before.

Soon after making my transformation I encountered my poor victim, Sir Danvers Carew, who was unfortunate enough to cross my path. As I heard him ask me politely for directions, I became impatient and irritable—for no good reason or cause on his part.

With a hysterical outburst, I clubbed the unsuspecting fool with my cane. As I committed this unforgivable crime, I was aware of a cold rush of terror coarsing through my veins. A light flickered somewhere inside me,

and I suddenly saw the consequences of what I had just done. Quickly, I fled from the scene.

I ran to the house in Soho and destroyed my papers, which contained evidence of my double life. Then I set out through the lamplit streets, gloating on my crime, yet still trembling at the idea that it had been done. Hyde had a song upon his lips as he mixed and drank the draught.

With streaming tears of gratitude and remorse, I fell upon my knees as Henry Jekyll. I could have screamed out loud. My mind was flooded with hideous images and sounds from my twisted memory. But I continued to cry and pray.

As the remorse faded, it was followed by a feeling of joy. After all, now I was confined to the body and mind of Dr. Jekyll. Hyde didn't have to be brought back, and oh, how I rejoiced to think it! I humbly embraced the restrictions of natural life! And with sincere determination I locked the door to my office and ground the key under my heel.

The next day, I heard the news of the murder cried out in the square. "Hyde is the culprit!" Jekyll was now my safety net. Should Hyde peep out for an instant, the hands of all men would be raised to capture him.

For my past sins, I resolved to be a better person. And I can say with honesty that my promises were fruitful. I can't say I got tired of this unselfish and innocent life. I think I enjoyed it more than ever. But as I fulfilled my promises, I began to feel less and less regretful.

Soon the darker side of me growled for attention as it had done before. Not that I even dreamed of bringing Hyde back to life—the very idea of it would bring the onset of a nervous breakdown. No, it was in the mind and body of Henry Jekyll that I was once more tempted to dabble in ill deeds. And so I did.

It was this brief failure that finally destroyed what was left of my soul. And yet, I was not alarmed. The fall seemed natural, like a return to the old days before I had made my discovery.

Chapter
13

THE FINAL TRANSFORMATION

*I*t was a fine, clear January day, frost melting on the ground and cloudless overhead. Regent's Park was full of sweet bird chirps and spring scents. I sat in the sun on a bench, the animal within me calm and satisfied for the moment. The angel in me promised to make up for it, but was not yet moved to begin. After all, I was like my neighbors. Then I smiled, comparing myself with others—my active good will to their lazy neglect. And at the very moment of that vain, yet glorious thought, a horrible nausea came over me and I began to shudder. These waves passed and left me feeling faint. All at once I was aware of a change in the temper of my thoughts.

Suddenly, there was a greater boldness and a lesser fear of danger. I looked down. My clothes hung on my shrunken limbs. The hand that lay on my knee was corded and hairy. I was once more Edward Hyde! A moment before I had been safe, respected, and admired. Now, I was hunted, homeless, and despised.

My reason wavered, but it did not fail me completely. In my second self, my senses seemed sharpened to a point. Therefore, in situations where Jekyll may have failed, Hyde rose to the importance of the moment. How was I to reach my drugs, which were in a drawer in my office? That was the problem Hyde set out to solve. I crushed my head in my hands.

I had shut and locked the laboratory door for good. There was no longer a key. If I tried to enter by the house, my own servants would have me captured. I realized I would need assistance and thought of Lanyon. How could I possibly persuade him? How could I even make my way to his house? Then I remembered that I could write in the handwriting of the good doctor! And once I had that spark of hope, the rest of the plan lit up on its own.

Catching a passing hansom cab, I drove to a hotel on Portland Street. At my appearance, which was indeed comical, the cab driver could not conceal his laughter. Until we reached the inn I kept

my self control. Then I whacked him with my new cane. The smile withered from his face.

As I entered the hotel I snarled at the staff, who kept their eyes averted from me. They obediently took my orders and led me to a private room. Here I would write my plea for help to Dr. Lanyon.

In danger of his life, Hyde was a new creature to me. He was shaken with extreme anger, his nerves high-strung. Yet the creature was clever, and controlled his fury with a great effort. He composed his two important letters, one to Lanyon and one to Poole, and sent them out.

From that point on, Hyde sat all day near the fire in his private room, gnawing his nails. There he dined, sitting alone with his fears. Then, when the sky had fallen completely black, he set forth in a cab towards Lanyon's house. That child of hell was inhuman. Nothing lived in him but fear and hatred. And when at last the driver dropped him on the corner of Lanyon's street, these two emotions raged within him like a tornado gathering wind and speed. He walked fast, hunted by his fears and chattering to himself. He was counting the minutes until midnight—still half an hour away.

When I came back to myself at Lanyon's, I realized another change had come over me. It was no longer the fear of being caught for murder, it was the horror of being Hyde that tormented me. I barely remember what was said to and by Lanyon. It was partly in a dream that I came home to my own house and got into bed. I fell into a deep sleep that even the racking nightmares couldn't break. I awoke in the morning shaken and weak, but refreshed. I still hated and feared the thought of the brute that slept within me, but I felt safe in the comfort of home, close to my drugs.

I was strolling leisurely across the courtyard after breakfast, when I was seized again with those painful sensations of change. I raced to my office, but could not stop Hyde from coming before I got there. It took a double dose of the elixir to bring me back to myself this time. But just six short hours later, the pangs returned and the drug had to be taken once more.

From that day forth, I was able to remain as Jekyll only under the immediate stimulation of the drug. At all hours of the day and night, I would feel the aching attacks of the metamorphosis. Above all, if I slept, or even dozed for a moment in my chair, I always awoke as Hyde. Under the continuous strain of this threatening doom I became ill. Fevers burned me up and my mind was occupied by only one thought—the horror of my other self. But when I slept, or when the medicine wore off, I would leap into images of terror. My body seemed too weak to contain the force of life.

The powers of Hyde seemed to have grown with the illness of Jekyll. Certainly, the hate that divided them was now equal on each side. Jekyll had seen the full deformity of the creature that shared some of his consciousness and would share his death. He saw Hyde as lifeless, though he possessed vital energy. It was shocking to Jekyll that this riffraff had a voice and could make gestures. And it was even more horrifying that this heartless beast was closer to him than a wife. Jekyll continuously felt Hyde struggling to be born, at the cost of his creator's own life.

The hatred of Hyde for Jekyll was different. His terror of being captured drove him to return to the body of Jekyll, but he loathed the need to do so. Hyde resented that the good doctor had turned on him. As punishment, he would burn my letters, scrawl on the pages of my books, and he destroyed the portrait of my father. Somehow though, when I think about how he fears my power to cut him off by suicide, I find it in my heart to pity him.

My tale now told, it is useless to go on about my suffering. No one has ever suffered such torments, let that be enough. My punishment might have gone on for years, if not for the last catastrophe which has now fallen. My supply of the drug, which had not been renewed since the first

experiment, began to run low. I sent for more and mixed the potion. The bubbling followed and the first change of color, but not the second. I drank it anyway, and nothing happened. Frightened at what would become of me, I asked Poole (as I'm sure he will tell you) to have London ransacked for a pure quantity of the original. It was in vain. I now realize that my first supply must have been impure, and that it was that unknown impurity which led the impossible to be possible.

About a week has gone by, and I am now finishing this statement under the influence of the last of the old powders. I write this as Henry Jekyll, esteemed doctor and friend. This, then, is the last time that Jekyll can think his own thoughts or see his own face in the mirror. Should the throes of change take me in the act of writing this, Hyde will tear it into pieces. I pray and I hope this does not happen so my story can be told by its true teller. Lanyon was too sickened by the events to relay an accurate version.

Indeed, the doom that is closing in on both myself and Hyde has already changed and crushed him. Half an hour from now I will again become the monster. I know he will sit, shuddering and weeping in my chair. Will he be captured and punished? As Jekyll, I no longer care what happens to Hyde, but I do wonder.

This is my true hour of death. Hyde will take over my soul and I will never again grace this earth as the good doctor. Here then, as I lay down the pen and proceed to seal up my confession, I bid you good-bye my dear friend, and hope you learn well from my misery. If that is all I can leave behind, it will be enough.

THE END

THE END

ABOUT THE AUTHOR

ROBERT LOUIS STEVENSON was born in Edinburgh, Scotland in 1850. He grew up a frail and sickly child.

His poor health later prevented him from a career in law. He turned to writing and traveled around the world in search of a remedy for his ill condition. On his travels he also met and married his wife.

After the success of *Treasure Island* in 1883, Stevenson wrote many different types of novels. He even took to writing grim, frightening tales such as *The Strange Case of Dr. Jekyll and Mr. Hyde.*

Spending his last years with his family on the South Pacific island of Samoa, Stevenson continued to write until his death in 1894 at the age of forty-four.

The Young Collector's
Illustrated Classics

The Adventures of Robin Hood
The Adventures of Tom Sawyer
Black Beauty
Call of the Wild
Dracula
Frankenstein
Gulliver's Travels
Heidi
Hunchback of Notre Dame
Little Women
Moby Dick
Oliver Twist
Peter Pan
The Prince and the Pauper
The Secret Garden
The Strange Case of Dr. Jekyll & Mr. Hyde
Swiss Family Robinson
Treasure Island
20,000 Leagues Under the Sea
White Fang

Masterwork Classics are available for special
and educational sales from:

Kidsbooks, Inc.
3535 West Peterson Avenue
Chicago, IL 60659
(773) 509-0707